WHY THE SUN AND THE MOON LIVE IN THE SKY

illustrations by Blair Lent

WHY THE SUN AND THE MOON LIVE IN THE SKY

an African folktale by Elphinstone Dayrell

HOUGHTON MIFFLIN COMPANY, BOSTON

ISBN: 0-395-06741-3 REGULAR EDITION

ISBN: 0-395-25381-0 SANDPIPER PAPERBOUND EDITION

G 10 9 8 7 6 5 4 3 2 1

Many years ago the sun and water were great friends, and both lived on the earth together. The sun very often used to visit the water, but the water never returned his visits. At last the sun asked the water why it was that he never came to see him in his house; the water replied that the sun's house was not big enough, and that if he came with his people he would drive the sun out.

The water then said, "If you wish me to visit you, you must build a very large house; but I warn you that it will have to be a very large place, as my people are very numerous, and take up a lot of room."

The sun promised to build a very large house, and soon afterwards he returned to his wife, the moon, who greeted him with a broad smile.

The sun told the moon what he had promised the water, and the next day began building a large house in which to entertain his friend.

When it was completed, he asked the water to come and
visit him.

When the water arrived, one of his people called out to the sun, and asked him whether it would be safe for the water to enter, and the sun answered, "Yes, tell my friend to come in."

The water then began to flow in, accompanied by the fish and all the water animals.

Very soon the water was knee-deep, so he asked the sun
if it was still safe, and the sun again said, "Yes," so
more of them came in.

When the water was level with the top of a man's head,
the water said to the sun, "Do you want more of my people
to come?"

And the sun and the moon both answered, "Yes," not knowing any better, so the water's people flowed on, until the sun and the moon had to perch themselves on top of the roof.

Again the water addressed the sun. He received the same answer so more of his people rushed in.

25

The water very soon overflowed the top of the roof, and the sun and moon were forced to go up into the sky, where they have remained ever since.

The End